Anna, Banana,

and the
Friendship
Split

Anna, Banana,
and the
Friendship
Split

Anica Mrose Rissi

ILLUSTRATED BY **Meg Park**

SIMON & SCHUSTER
BOOKS FOR YOUNG READERS

New York   London   Toronto   Sydney   New Delhi

SIMON & SCHUSTER BOOKS FOR YOUNG READERS
An imprint of Simon & Schuster Children's Publishing Division
1230 Avenue of the Americas, New York, New York 10020

For information about special discounts for bulk purchases, please contact Simon &
Schuster Special Sales at 1-866-506-1949 or business@simonandschuster.com.
The Simon & Schuster Speakers Bureau can bring authors to your live event. For more
information or to book an event, contact the Simon & Schuster Speakers Bureau at
1-866-248-3049 or visit our website at www.simonspeakers.com.
Book design by Laurent Linn
The text for this book is set in Minister Std.
The illustrations for this book are rendered digitally.
Manufactured in the United States of America
0116 FFG
4 6 8 10 9 7 5 3
Library of Congress Cataloging-in-Publication Data
Rissi, Anica Mrose.
Anna, Banana, and the friendship split / Anica Mrose Rissi; illustrated by Meg Park.

pages cm
Summary: Anna and Sadie have always been best friends so when Sadie suddenly starts
being mean, Anna is very sad and seeks support from her dog, Banana, and classmate
Isabel, as well as advice from her brother, Chuck, and her parents.
ISBN 978-1-4814-1605-4 (hardcover)
ISBN 978-1-4814-1607-8 (eBook)
1. Best friends—Fiction. 2. Friendship—Fiction. 3. Behavior—Fiction.
4. Schools—Fiction. 5. Family life—Fiction. 6. Dogs—Fiction.] I. Park, Meg, illustrator.
II. Title.
PZ7.R5265Ann 2015
[Fic]—dc23
2014006375

For Anna Luiza
(and Arugula, of course)

and the
Friendship
Split

Chapter One
Make a Wish

Sadie says the best thing about birthdays is getting presents, but my favorite part is the birthday wish. I've read all the fairy tales—I know you have to be careful what you wish for—so this year, I planned my wish out weeks in advance. I was ready.

Everyone sang as Dad brought out the cake and placed it on the picnic blanket spread across our living room floor. It was chocolate cake with pink vanilla frosting: Sadie's and my favorite. Nine yellow candles flickered on top.

I opened my mouth to suck in a huge breath,

when Mom startled me. "Banana!" she said. "Get your nose out of there! Cake is not for dogs."

Banana backed away from the birthday cake, making guilty eyes. She wagged her whole backside to tell Mom *sorry* and turned to sniff my best friend, Sadie, instead.

Sadie giggled and pulled Banana onto her lap. "Come on, Anna," she said to me. "Make a wish!"

I closed my eyes for just a second and pictured what I wanted: a trip to Water World. I could almost feel myself racing down a tall, twisty waterslide, zipping around the curves with Sadie right behind me, and splash-landing together in the giant wave pool below. The commercials made it look like the funnest place on Earth, and I'd been wanting to go since forever. Chuck had said our parents would never take us there, but

I knew if I used my birthday wish on it, it would have to come true. Birthday wishes have extra magic. That's how I got Banana.

I leaned toward the candles, ready to blow. But before I could let out my breath, Sadie whispered, "Wish for a pony."

I froze. Where would we keep a pony?

"Any day now, monkey face," Chuck said, sticking his finger in the frosting.

Ugh. For a second I considered using my wish to ask for a less-annoying older brother, but even birthday-wish magic probably couldn't fix Chuck.

Sadie nudged me. She snorted and flared her nostrils like the horses we'd seen at the park, and gave a little whinny of encouragement. She sounded just like a real stallion.

I grinned at her and Banana and turned back to my cake. Blowing out the candles with one big breath, I thought, *I wish for a pony.*

I can never say no to Sadie. She's my best friend.

Chapter Two

No Horsing Around

It's dumb to feel sad while eating pink cake, so I tried not to think about wasting my wish. Still, I knew I'd blown it. I would love to have a pony, but that last-second wish would never come true. And even if a pony somehow magically appeared in our living room, there was no way Mom and Dad would let me keep it. Not even if I trained it to sweep the floors with its tail and mow the lawn with its teeth and bring us all breakfast in bed. Not even if I said *please*.

For a minute I imagined keeping a secret pony in my room, but that didn't work so well for

Chuck and the class hamster, and it's much, much harder to hide a horse. Even the smallest pony would barely fit in my closet, and all my dresses would get wrinkled and start smelling like hay. And even if I managed to hide a whole horse, how would I hide the manure?

Maybe I shouldn't have listened to Sadie, but she's usually full of good ideas. It was her idea to make my birthday party a picnic, with a checkered blanket and a thermos of strawberry lemonade and little tea sandwiches all packed in a basket. When I woke up to rain, I thought the party would be ruined, but Sadie saved the day.

She said it would be even more fun to have the picnic inside, and surprised me with a handful of plastic ants. It was a perfect party, except for my wish. Just this once, I should have ignored Sadie and stuck with my plan.

I let Banana lick the last of the frosting off my fingers while Sadie made a line of ants march toward the leftovers and Dad and Chuck cleared the empty plates. Normally clearing the dishes is my job too, but Dad said the birthday princess gets a day off from chores.

"Then I guess I'm the birthday princess *every* day," Sadie said, tossing her curls out of her face.

It was true. At her dad's house, Sadie doesn't have to do anything and she still gets an allowance. She's supposed to make her bed every morning at her mom's, but usually she forgets and the housekeeper does it for her. Her mom doesn't even notice. Sadie's so lucky that way. Her parents let her do whatever she wants.

"Well, when you're at our house, you're welcome to help pitch in," my mom said.

I expected Sadie to say, "No thanks," but instead she got up off the floor and started gathering the wrapping paper and ribbons I'd taken off my presents. I felt lame being the only one not helping, so I straightened my party hat, kissed Banana's snout, and got up too.

"Here," Sadie said. "You need more birthday bling." She reached over and tied a gold ribbon around my wrist to match the one she'd already put on Banana's collar. Then she stuck a silver bow to her forehead. "How do I look?" she asked, crossing her eyes, lifting her chin, and posing like a fashion model.

"Fancy," I said. We cracked up and I felt a hundred times better. Sadie's so silly. She always knows how to make me laugh.

I picked up some crumpled tissue paper that Banana was nosing and saw a small, wrapped present underneath. "What's this?" I asked, holding it out for Mom to see.

"Oh!" Mom said. "I forgot that one. It's from Nana and Grumps. Go ahead, open it."

I untied the ribbon and peeled the tape off

the shiny paper, being very careful not to rip it. Inside was a dark velvet box like the one that holds Mom's favorite earrings.

My heart went tense and buzzy with excitement, like a wind-up toy about to be released.

I opened the box. Sadie gasped.

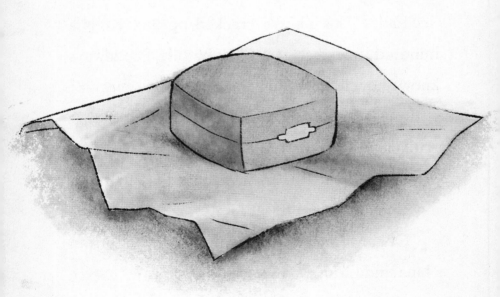

Chapter Three
Surprise, Surprise

"It's a pony!" Sadie squealed, reaching for the box. But I held on to it and stared at the necklace inside. It was a pony pendant on a thin gold chain. The pony had one hoof lifted, ready to trot. Its bright blue jewel of an eye sparkled and danced in the light. I had never seen anything so beautiful.

My smile was so big I could almost feel it in my toes. My birthday wish had come true!

"Try it on, Anna," Dad said. I held up my hair while he fastened the chain around my neck. I stood up a little straighter. I felt instantly older.

"Lovely," Mom said, nodding her approval. "Very elegant." I ran to the mirror and looked. It was perfect. Even Banana looked impressed.

"That's so pretty! Let me try it," Sadie said, coming up behind me.

"In a minute," I said.

Sadie did not look pleased.

Chuck sniffed loudly. "Pee-yew," he said, fanning the air in front of his nose. "Something smells like horse poop. Anna, is that you?"

I stuck out my tongue at him and grabbed Sadie's hand. "Come on, let's go play in my room."

We raced up the stairs with Banana at our heels. "Don't start any big projects," my mom called after us. "Sadie's mother will be here any minute now."

"Unless she forgot me again," Sadie muttered as we tumbled into my bedroom.

"I'm sure she didn't," I said, but of course we both remembered the time that happened. My mom says Sadie's mom is a little distracted these days because of the divorce. Sadie doesn't say much about it.

I plopped down on the rug and tossed Banana's favorite chew toy, a yellow plastic bunny, across the room. Banana scampered after it. "Chuck is so annoying," I said.

Sadie shrugged. "I think he's funny."

"*What?*" I shrieked. "He's not funny, he's gross. And rude. You don't know how lucky you are to be an only child."

Banana dropped the toy in Sadie's lap. She threw it into the hall, and Banana ran off again. "Well, when we grow up, I'm going to marry him," Sadie announced.

I stared at her. She couldn't be serious. "Ew. No you're not."

"Yes I am," she said. "And then you and I will be sisters. And we'll live next door to each other in two big mansions with one gigantic pool across both our backyards. And I'll have a huge stable full of beautiful horses, so we can go riding every day."

"Okay," I said. "But we could do that even if you don't marry Chuck. If you marry him, you'll have to *kiss* him. That's like kissing dirty socks." I wrinkled my nose at the thought.

Sadie ignored me and took the rabbit back from Banana. "My mansion will have a special room for Banana that's filled with dog toys, and a servant whose only job is to toss them for her. And another servant who gives her belly rubs all day and night." She held the rabbit just out of Banana's reach so Banana had to jump for it. I wanted to snatch the toy out of Sadie's hand so she'd quit teasing Banana, but I couldn't move. Sadie was being weird, and I didn't like her pulling Banana into it. The whole thing was making me nervous. Banana jumped and jumped, and let out a desperate yip.

"But Banana is my dog," I said. "She'll live with me."

"She's Chuck's dog too," Sadie said. She squeezed the yellow bunny, making it squeak.

My chest felt tight. I wasn't sure why we were fighting about this, and I was even less sure how to stop it. "But I picked Banana out. And I named her. And I do all her walks and feeding and stuff, and she sleeps in my room." I tried to pull Banana onto my lap, but she wriggled away and lunged for the toy in Sadie's fist. "Chuck wanted to name her *Weenie*."

"Well, Banana can choose where to live," Sadie said. "But I'm sure she'll like my house better, since I'll be richer and have more servants and stuff."

I swallowed at the giant lump in my throat. I didn't feel like a birthday princess anymore. I didn't even feel like a birthday *peasant*. I just felt terrible.

Sadie dropped the dog toy and climbed to her

feet. "My turn to wear the necklace now."

I looked up at my best friend. She scowled down at me. I didn't know why Sadie was acting so mad, but I knew I would do anything to fix it.

Chapter Four
Pony Up

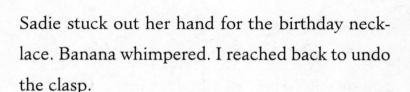

Sadie stuck out her hand for the birthday necklace. Banana whimpered. I reached back to undo the clasp.

I watched as Sadie put on my necklace and studied herself in the mirror. The pony pendant shimmered against Sadie's red top. It looked magical. Sadie looked pleased.

"That looks great," I said, because it was true, and because I wanted Sadie to like me again.

Sadie nodded. "It does," she said. "I love it. You should give it to me."

"What?" I squeaked like Banana's toy. Banana's ears shot up in surprise.

"You should give me the necklace," Sadie repeated. "It's half mine anyway, since I'm the one who said you should wish for it."

"But . . . but I can't," I said. My heart was beating fast, but my brain felt slow, like it couldn't keep up with Sadie's logic. I tried to explain. "It's my birthday present. I just got it. Nana and Grumps haven't even seen me wear it yet."

"Fine," Sadie said, but it didn't sound fine. "Then I get Banana."

"No!" I said. I thought my heart might gallop right out of my chest. There was no way I could choose between my dog and my best friend. They were the two most important things I had.

"Sadie, stop. Please stop. It's my birthday. Don't be mean."

Sadie glared straight at me and crossed her arms. I'd never seen her look so angry. I stared down at the carpet and tried not to cry.

"I thought you were my friend," Sadie said. Her words felt like punches.

"I am!" I said. "I'm your best friend. And you're mine."

"Well, you're not acting like it," she shot back. "Best friends are supposed to share everything. I would let you wear any of my necklaces."

I knew she would. Sadie had about a million necklaces and they were all beautiful. "But it's not the same," I said, desperate to make her see. "Yours aren't that special." Sadie's mouth dropped open in surprise and I knew I had said the exact wrong thing. "I mean—"

"You're so selfish, Anna," Sadie said. Her cheeks were all splotchy like they sometimes get when she's holding back tears. She turned away.

"Anna!" my dad shouted up to us. "Sadie's mom is here! Time to say good-bye!"

But we didn't say good-bye. Sadie tucked the necklace under her shirt, yanked off her birthday hat and dropped it on the floor, and marched past me without saying another word. I listened as she went downstairs and walked out the door.

I had no idea how everything had gone so wrong.

Banana nosed at my hand and gave it two quick licks, but I pulled away. Not even my dog could make me feel better now.

I threw myself onto the bed and cried. I wished this birthday had never happened.

Chapter Five

Plan-tastic

My Nana always says, "Everything looks brighter in the morning light." Well, she was wrong. The morning after my birthday picnic was still stormy and dark. My tummy felt sick over the fight with Sadie. One stupid wish and I'd lost my one and only best friend forever.

I couldn't believe she'd stormed off like that, and taken my necklace, too. It wasn't like her to get so mad, and I had no idea how to set things right. Part of me wasn't even sure I wanted to. I thought she should be the one to apologize to me. But I knew she thought that I'd been mean too, and that made me feel extra terrible.

I sat at the breakfast table, pushing the Gorilla Grams around in my cereal bowl and ignoring the disgusting sounds Chuck was making with his orange juice. It's like boys are born with a gift for grossness. If grossness were an Olympic sport, Chuck would be a gold medalist for sure. They'd probably give him the gold, the silver, *and* the bronze. He's that talented.

My dad walked into the kitchen, straightening his tie. Even though Dad is a writer and he only has to commute to his desk right here in our house, he still gets dressed up for work every day like he used to do when he worked in a real office. Mom says if she worked from home she would never take off her bathrobe and bunny slippers, but apparently the tie helps Dad focus. And Mom doesn't own any bunny slippers, so I guess maybe that's some kind of joke.

"Good morning, kiddos. Any big plans for the school day?" Dad asked as he poured himself some coffee. Chuck burped in response and broke into giggles. He was lucky Mom wasn't in the room.

I shook my head no and kept poking at the cereal. Then I looked up. *A plan! Of course*. That was exactly what I needed. Things always go better when there's a plan. Like when Sadie's dad took us to the county fair and we made a list first of all the rides we wanted to go on so we wouldn't miss out on any of the best ones, and had the most fun ever. Or like the time Sadie and I got lost in the mall, but I didn't panic because Mom had said if that ever happened I should meet her at the information booth. Or like how, if I'd only stuck to my birthday-wish plan, Sadie and I wouldn't be fighting.

If I had a plan, I could stop wondering what to do. I'd just follow the plan and get my best friend back. Then she'd be nice again.

I took a bite of soggy cereal and thought while I chewed. At my feet, Banana tilted her head to one side like she was thinking hard too.

The easiest plan would be to build a time

machine and go back to before the fight ever happened, but I wasn't sure I could do that without Sadie's help. If I could find a real pony to give her to keep, that would probably make Sadie happy, but it wouldn't really fix whatever had gotten her so mad in the first place. Besides, there wasn't enough time to find a pony before I had to leave for school. I needed this plan to be simple. I tried to think of the simplest plan possible. By the time I'd swallowed the last spoonful of Gorilla Grams, I knew how to fix things with Sadie.

The plan was this: I had to tell Sadie I was sorry. Even though I wasn't sure exactly what I'd done wrong, I could still apologize, since I definitely was sorry that Sadie was mad. And after I said sorry, I would give her the necklace. The necklace was mine, and it was special, but Sadie meant a bazillion times more to me than any necklace could. Besides, knowing Sadie, she'd probably let me borrow it.

I'd set the plan in motion as soon as I got to school. Sadie would say sorry too, we'd both be forgiven, and everything would go back to normal. Since I was letting her keep the necklace, she'd forget about taking Banana. Maybe it would even stop raining in time for recess, and we could try out my new birthday jump rope from Chuck. I would let Sadie skip with it first, to show her what a good friend I can be. To show her I'm not selfish.

Banana looked up hopefully and thumped her tail against the kitchen floor. I tossed her a stray Gorilla Gram and crossed my fingers for luck. The plan *had* to work.

Chapter Six

Hurry Up and Wait

When I got to school, I went straight to my classroom, since it was too rainy for the playground. Sadie wasn't there yet. Usually she gets to school first because her bus arrives early and Chuck and I walk, but today Mom drove us. I don't mind walking to school in the rain, because I have purple boots and a polka-dot umbrella. But Chuck hates wearing a raincoat, and Mom hates hearing him whine.

I said good morning to Ms. Burland, who was writing the word of the day on the board.

Ms. Burland is the best teacher in the entire Lower School. She turns every lesson into a story and always assigns fun projects. She's young and pretty and wears colorful shoes that she buys in places like Boston and New York City. Today her shoes were bright green, with square toes and silver buckles. The word she was writing on the whiteboard was "perky." *Perky: cheerful and lively.* I said the word softly to myself and liked the popping feel of it in my mouth. It seemed like a good sign.

I sat at my desk and lined up my pencils while I waited for Sadie to arrive. I have a regular yellow pencil for regular old schoolwork. That one goes at the top of the desk. Then comes the lucky blue pencil that I use for spelling tests and math quizzes. Below that, I put my favorite pencil, the

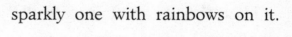

sparkly one with rainbows on it. That one is so special, I hardly ever use it. I just line it up with the others because I love to look at it.

Kids came into the class-room, shaking wet hair and shrugging off raincoats. The room got loud with their voices, but I tuned everyone out and kept my eyes on the door. I especially tuned out Justin, who sits in the desk behind mine and is always kicking my chair or tugging my ponytail or asking stupid questions like is my refrigerator still running, so he can make a dumb joke about how I'd better go catch it. Sadie once said she thinks Justin is cute, but she's never had to hear him burp her whole name, first, middle, and last. Banana and I think Justin's disgusting.

I looked at the clock, then back at the door. Still no Sadie. Maybe her bus was late.

Oh no. What if she wasn't coming to school today? What if she was so mad at me, she was never coming back? Maybe she'd told her mom about our fight and her mom had let her change schools. Maybe they were moving to a whole new town. What if Sadie disappeared and I never got to see her again?

I jumped out of my chair. Just then, Sadie slipped into the classroom and the first bell rang. My heart flooded with relief.

"Sadie!" I said, but she didn't look at me. She walked right past me like I wasn't even there.

I sank into my seat. This wasn't part of the plan.

Chapter Seven

Pretty Please with a Pony on Top

Ms. Burland clapped twice to start the day, and everyone scrambled to their desks. I stared at the back of Sadie's head, two rows over and one row up. I had to get her attention.

"Sadie," I whispered just loud enough for her to hear, but she didn't turn around. She inched her chair to the right, moving even farther away from me. "Sadie!" I said a little louder. Ms. Burland shot me a warning glance as she started the morning lesson. I clamped my mouth shut.

Now what was I going to do?

I watched in horror as Sadie leaned over her

desk and whispered something to Amanda, the girl who sits in front of her. Amanda glanced at me, then whispered back to Sadie. Sadie giggled softly.

I couldn't believe it. Sadie never whispered with Amanda. Sadie hardly ever even *talked* to Amanda. Amanda sometimes picked her nose in public! My best friend was whispering with a

known nose-picker and she refused to even look at me. It felt like I'd swallowed a bucket of rocks.

I had to do something. I had to follow the plan and apologize before it was too late. Before Sadie hated me forever, and made Amanda and everyone else in the entire third grade hate me too.

I reached into my desk and pulled out a notebook. Flipping to a blank page, I picked up my superspecial sparkly rainbow pencil and wrote:

Dear Sadie,
I'm sorry. Please don't hate me. You can have the necklace if you'll be my friend again.

Love,
Anna

P.S. If it isn't raining, we can try my new jump rope at recess.

I drew a little picture of Banana at the bottom, then ripped out the message and folded it up small. I waited until Ms. Burland turned around to write something on the whiteboard, then I tossed the note across the room, onto Sadie's desk. She covered it quickly with her palm and swept it onto her lap.

I held my breath while Sadie unfolded the note under her desk. She stared at it for what felt like hours, before picking up her pen.

I exhaled. She was writing back. She was talking to me again. It was going to be okay.

Sadie refolded the note slowly, keeping her eyes on the teacher the whole time. She reached behind her and handed the note to Timothy, who handed it across to Isabel, who passed it over to me.

I unfolded it and read what Sadie had written.

Dear Anna,
<u>NO</u>. We are not friends.
And the necklace is mine.
Sadie
P.S. Who needs your stupid jump rope.

Chapter Eight
Sorry Isn't Enough

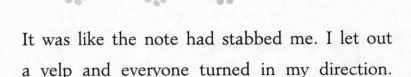

It was like the note had stabbed me. I let out a yelp and everyone turned in my direction. Everyone, including Ms. Burland.

"Anna!" Ms. Burland said. "Are you passing notes?"

"No!" I said. I looked over at Sadie, and her eyes were shooting daggers right at me. I knew what she was thinking: that if Ms. Burland read the note, we'd *both* be caught. I had to act fast. I crumpled up the paper, shoved it into my mouth, and chewed as hard as I could.

"Anna!" Ms. Burland said, sounding as

shocked as I felt. "Spit that out!" I kept chewing.
The note tasted disgusting, but I had to destroy
the evidence. *"Now,"* Ms. Burland ordered.

Tears pricked my eyes as I spit the soggy,
chewed-up wad onto my desk. I'd never dis-
obeyed a teacher like that, especially not Ms.
Burland.

Everyone started talking at once.

"Ew!"

"Gross!"

"She ate it!"

"Awesome!"

Sadie stayed silent, her arms folded across her chest.

"Enough!" Ms. Burland barked. The class went still. "Anna, please throw that mess away. You'll be staying in for the next two recesses with your head down on your desk. You know better than to pass notes during class."

My cheeks burned. If I had a tail like Banana's, I'd have tucked it between my legs in shame. Two recesses! I had never been in so much trouble. Not even close. Ms. Burland was my favorite teacher, and I'd never be able to look her in the eye again. It was only late September and already I'd ruined the whole school year. I knew what she thought I was now: a troublemaker. A troublemaker who was one prank away from landing in the principal's office. A troublemaker who ought to be locked up in jail and sentenced to ten years of hard labor and extra homework.

But at least I'd saved Sadie. At least I'd proven that I wasn't a snitch. And without my best friend to play with, there was no point to having recess anyway.

Ms. Burland continued the lesson, but I didn't hear a word of it. I wiped the tears off my face and scraped up what was left of the note. I could feel everyone watching me as I carried it to the front of the classroom and dropped it into the trash. It landed with a wet *thwunk*.

I turned and walked back to my seat, keeping my head down. I didn't look at Sadie, *couldn't* look at Sadie, but still—a flash of gold from her direction caught my eye.

I looked. It was the necklace. *My* necklace, hanging from Sadie's neck. She was twisting and twirling it around one finger, and smiling the nastiest smile I'd ever seen.

All of a sudden, I felt furious. Nothing about this moment was fair. I'd lost my recess and I'd lost my necklace and I'd lost my best friend. I wanted to leap over the desks and take back my necklace and shove that mean smile right off Sadie's face. But of course I couldn't do that. There was nothing I could do but sit back down and wait for the world to end.

I stepped forward and heard a loud *crack*. I looked down. My favorite sparkly rainbow pencil lay on the floor beneath my foot, snapped in two.

This was officially the worst day of my life.

Chapter Nine
Wish Again

Sitting through recess with my head on my desk, I made a decision: I was never coming back to school again. I would stay home every day and read tons of books and learn to speak dog, and Banana would be my best and only friend. Maybe if I promised to do lots of extra chores, my parents would let me drop out of third grade.

Or maybe not.

I needed a foolproof way to get out of school. I needed another wish.

That night, I saw my chance. Dad had roasted a chicken for dinner, and when Chuck and I broke the wishbone, I closed my eyes and wished for a blizzard, even though we never get snow days at this time of year. But it didn't matter what I'd wished for. Chuck got the bigger half.

When I went upstairs to brush my teeth, I stuck my head out the bath- room window and searched the sky for a falling star. But there were no stars to wish on. It was still raining. And now my hair was wet.

I stood in front of the mirror and blinked hard, again and again and again. I blinked until I was dizzy, then blinked some more, but no lucky eyelash fell out. I would have to find something else to wish on.

I pulled one of Banana's long, silky, brown ears. "If I rub your belly like Aladdin's magic lamp, will you grant me a wish?" I asked. Banana looked skeptical.

I put on my pajamas and climbed into bed. Banana flopped down in her basket beside me and heaved a loud, doggy sigh. I guess my misery was contagious.

Contagious! That gave me an idea.

Hearing my mom's footsteps coming up the stairs, I curled up on my side and tried to look weak. Mom sat on my bed and stroked my hair like she always does when she tucks me in. Suddenly, it was hard not to cry again.

"You okay, Annabear?" Mom asked. "You seem a little down tonight."

I shut my eyes to block the tears. Part of me wanted to tell Mom everything, even the part about getting in trouble with Ms. Burland. But I knew I couldn't. I had to try my other plan.

"No," I told her. "I'm not okay. I think I'm

getting sick. Very sick. I probably can't go to school tomorrow. I might even have to miss the whole rest of the year."

Mom went still. "Is that so?" she said.

"Yes," I choked out. I gave a little cough, hoping it sounded fatal.

Mom moved her hand from my hair to my forehead. "You don't have a fever," she said, "and your skin isn't clammy. I bet you're going to be just fine."

Oh no. Mom knew I was lying. Now I really did feel sick.

"Did something bad happen at school today, Anna?" she asked.

"No," I mumbled. "I just thought I might be getting the flu."

Mom kissed me, leaned down to kiss Banana, too, then stood. "Well, let's see how you feel in the morning. You'd be amazed what a good night's sleep can cure."

Yeah, right, I thought as she turned out the light. Nothing could cure what had happened with Sadie. Nothing.

Chapter Ten

Mean, Meaner, Meanest

The next day, the rain stopped, but the misery did not. It only got worse.

First, Chuck poured himself all the Gorilla Grams, which he *knows* is my favorite breakfast, so I had to eat plain old Oatie O's instead. When I complained just a little, Mom snapped at me for whining about it.

Next, Dad asked why I wasn't wearing my new necklace. "Oh," I said, trying to think fast. "It, um, it doesn't go with this shirt."

Chuck slurped at his cereal. "Mmmm," he

said, "Gorilla Grams are *soooooo* good." And then I got in trouble for screaming.

Nobody was on my side.

At school, Sadie didn't even bother to whisper about me or glare anymore. She just pretended I didn't exist. I stuck out my tongue at the back of her head. It didn't help.

I was so upset, I couldn't focus on a single word Ms. Burland was saying. It was like my brain had been replaced with a thick glob of oatmeal, and no thoughts could swim through the sticky, gooey mush. When she called on me to read aloud from the top of page twenty-four, I got through two whole sentences—"The wonderful world of fungi includes the tasty mushrooms you find in your omelet and the itchy fungus that grows on your feet. But that's not all!"—before I realized the entire class was laughing at me.

"Anna," Ms. Burland said, "pay attention. We finished with science five minutes ago. Please take out your geography book." I wished I had long ears like Banana's so I could hide my face behind them.

When it was time for our spelling and vocabulary test, Ms. Burland walked between the rows of desks, calling out words in a dramatic voice, like she was announcing them to the guests at a royal banquet. I'd memorized every single word over the weekend with my dad, but now they went in one ear and out the other. It was the worst I'd done on any test, ever. Not even my lucky blue pencil could save me from failing.

It was almost a relief when recess came and everyone else ran outside to play while I pressed my cheek to the desk.

I decided the best way to get through lunch again was to sit at a far table with my back to the room so I wouldn't have to see Sadie not being my friend—or, worse, being friends with anyone else. I ate my cheese sandwich and kept my eyes down and pretended I was invisible, same as yesterday. I didn't even look up when Justin pointed at my napkin and said, "Hey, Anna, aren't you going to eat that? Yummy, yummy paper." I didn't care what Justin said anyway. The only thing I cared about was losing my best friend.

After lunch, I stared at Sadie's back while Ms. Burland handed out a worksheet on fractions. I wished I had my necklace back. I wished I had a real pony, or maybe a Pegasus, so I could gallop off and fly to a castle in the sky, and never have to watch Sadie ignoring me again. Or so the pony could kick her.

Enough.

I couldn't take the silent treatment any longer. "Sadie," I hissed.

Sadie didn't react.

"Sadie!" I whispered again, and finally she turned around.

The necklace gleamed. Her eyes narrowed. My stomach clenched.

"Did you hear something?" Sadie said to Isabel, who sits in the desk next to mine.

Isabel looked at Sadie, then at me, then back at Sadie. "Yes," she said. "I heard Anna say your name."

Sadie wrinkled her nose. "Oh," she said. "Well, I didn't hear anything." She whirled back around.

"Thanks," I whispered to Isabel. She shrugged like it was no big deal, but it felt like the first time anyone besides Banana had been nice to me in years.

Even though Sadie was acting so mean, I

wouldn't really have let a pony kick her. I missed her. I missed our sharing secrets and making each other laugh and finishing each other's sentences and being a pair. I missed how being with her made everything more exciting. As mad as I was, I would forgive her in a second if she'd forgive me back. I just wanted us to make up and have fun again.

I looked up at the whiteboard and read the word of the day.

Yearn: to ache for.

Yeah. It felt like that.

Chapter Eleven
Push Comes to Shove

Walking home from school, I dragged behind Chuck, kicking at the sidewalk with each step. A rock popped up off my shoe and bounced into Chuck's calf. "Ow!" he said, shooting me a glare. "Watch it."

Great. Now my brother hated me too.

"What's your problem, grumpy-pants?" he asked.

I stared down at my feet and watched the right one land smack in the middle of a sidewalk crack. Sadie says stepping on cracks is bad luck. Well, fine. I stomped on the next one with my left foot, daring my luck to just try to get worse.

"Sadie and I had a fight," I told Chuck. "She hates me. She won't even talk to me. And she took my pony necklace." As horrible as it was to admit the truth, it also felt good to tell someone. Even if that someone was stupid old Chuck.

"So?" he said. "Take it back."

"Take *what* back?" I said. "I didn't do anything. She just hates me."

Chuck rolled his eyes. "Take the necklace back, dummy."

"I *can't* take the necklace back because it's AROUND HER NECK!" I screamed. "She stole it from me and she wants to steal Banana, too, and she *hates* me and she's *not speaking to me* and she's supposed to be my *best friend* and I don't even know what I did!"

"Yeesh, stop yelling," Chuck said. "You don't have to be so dramatic about it."

My head popped off. Almost. "DID YOU HEAR ME? I LOST MY BEST FRIEND!"

He shrugged.

I crossed my arms tight across my chest to stop them from flailing around so much. Chuck was making me feel ridiculous.

"So get a new best friend," he said. "Or pretend you're not a total wuss and stick up for yourself for once."

"Argh!" I shrieked. And then I shoved him.

Chuck laughed and started walking again. "See? Sometimes you have to push back, Annabean."

"I'm not a bean," I grumbled. But I couldn't help wondering if maybe Chuck was right.

Chapter Twelve
Dressed to Kill

The next morning, I got up before anyone else in the house. Even Banana stayed curled up in her basket, with one ear flopped over the side. Her eyes followed my every move as I stomped around the room, getting ready for school. Getting ready to grow a spine. Getting ready to stand up to Sadie.

I yanked open a dresser drawer and dug for the perfect outfit. I pulled out a purple shirt with three bows on the front. "This," I explained to Banana, "is the top that Sadie says I should never wear because it makes me look like a giant grape." I tossed my pajamas onto the floor and put the shirt on.

Banana nosed at her blanket a little nervously but kept her eyes on me.

"And this," I told her, stepping into my favorite skirt, "is the perfect thing to wear with it. Sadie says purple and orange clash."

Banana shoved her snout all the way under the blanket. But *I* wasn't afraid. I turned to the mirror. Orange with purple looked pretty great. But the outfit still needed a finishing touch.

I brushed out my hair and slid on the pink headband Sadie had given me for my birthday. The one she'd gotten for herself, too, so we could be twins. She would see it in my hair today, above my orange skirt and grapey top, and she'd know I was wearing this outfit for her. She'd know I was wearing it because I was no longer trying to be her best friend.

Mom knocked softly and pushed open my bedroom door. "Anna, time to wake—oh! You're already up. Well, don't you look nice."

I twirled and my skirt flared out around me. I felt pretty. I felt Sadie-proof. I felt ready.

"Come down for breakfast, then," Mom said. "There's even time for pancakes."

Banana leaped out of her basket, wiggling with excitement from snout to tail. I followed her downstairs.

I didn't have to wish for things to get better. I was making it happen myself.

Chapter Thirteen
Color Wars

I didn't even look for Sadie on the playground before school, and I kept not looking for her when I got to our classroom. I had no idea if she was still ignoring my existence. I was ignoring hers first.

Besides, I was busy. Wednesday mornings are the best mornings because that's when we have art. It was easy to forget about Sadie when I had something fun to focus on.

Today Ms. Burland showed us some famous paintings of animals, like a tiger crouching in the jungle and a flamingo with a long, silly neck.

There was even one of a herd of buffalo that a caveman had drawn on the wall of his cave.

Ms. Burland passed out oil pastels so we could draw our favorite animals in their natural habitats. I'd been going to do a portrait of Banana in her basket, but then I'd gotten a better idea. So far, it was turning out great.

I looked down at the paper on my desk and reached for a copper stick. The unicorn I was drawing was about to get shiny hoofs.

"There," I said out loud as I finished coloring them in. I looked up to see if anyone had noticed how fancy my picture was. Isabel leaned over to see.

"Ooh, nice," she said. "I like all the colors in his mane."

"Thank you," I said. I peeked at the project on her desk. She'd drawn a dolphin leaping out of the ocean waves. Above him, stars sparkled in a black sky. The stars were made from real glitter. "Wow," I told her. "You're super talented."

Isabel shrugged, but it was true. She was probably the best artist in our class, and maybe the best in the entire third grade.

I glanced at the supplies scattered across her desk and suddenly I knew exactly what my picture needed. "Can I use some of that purple glitter?" I asked. "Please?"

As Isabel handed me the glitter glue, Sadie whipped around in her seat. "Purple?" Sadie said, loud enough for the whole room to hear. "I hope you're not using that with *orange*."

I lifted my chin. This was the moment I'd been waiting for. "What do you care?" I shot back.

"I don't," Sadie said. "I don't care what you do. I just don't like looking at things that are ugly."

Hot anger prickled up my neck and spread all the way to the tips of my ears. "So don't look," I said. "Nobody asked you."

Sadie blinked with surprise, then shoved her hand into the air. "Ms. Burland?" she said, without waiting to be called on. "Don't you think that purple and orange clash?"

Ms. Burland looked up from the tests she was grading. "Not at all," she said. "In fact, look." She stuck out one leg and pulled back her pant cuff to show us the suede purple shoe and orange-with-purple-polka-dots sock she was wearing.

I let out my breath.

"Cool," Isabel said.

"Thanks," Ms. Burland replied.

Sadie hunched back over her drawing and didn't say another word.

Chapter Fourteen
Skip, Hop, and a Jump

At recess, I took my new jump rope out to the playground and grabbed another from the equipment bin. I found Isabel sitting cross-legged on a rock, reading a book. "Wanna play?" I asked.

Isabel glanced up. "Definitely," she said.

I took a few practice skips while Isabel climbed down from the rock. My rope hit the ground with a satisfying *smack, smack*. I couldn't help smiling as I jumped over it.

"Do you know 'One, Two, Buckle My Shoe'?" I asked.

She picked up the other jump rope. "Yeah, but it's more fun if we make up our own rhyme."

I stopped skipping. "About what?"

"Anything! There aren't any rules. We just make stuff up."

No rules? This was going to be very different from playing with Sadie.

Isabel kept talking. "It could be about what's for lunch or places we want to travel or animals or wizards or school or just nonsense words."

"Okay," I said. "Let's do one about food. I'm hungry."

We swung our ropes and jumped in unison. Isabel chanted to the rhythm: "One, two, blueberry stew! Three, four, make us some more."

My turn. "Five, six, please no fish sticks. Seven, eight, 'cause those we hate."

Isabel grinned. "Nine, ten, tacos again? Eleven, twelve, eat those yourself!"

"Thirteen, fourteen . . ." I paused and missed a beat. "Uh, what food rhymes with fourteen?"

We broke into giggles. "Hmm. S'more-teen?" Isabel said, making a silly face. "Start another one!"

I couldn't believe I'd been sitting next to Isabel for almost a month and had no idea she was so much fun.

We jumped and I started a new rhyme. "One, two, doggies make poo. Three, four, ponies make more!"

Isabel laughed so hard she almost fell over.

"That's not how it goes," a familiar voice sneered behind me.

I whirled around and saw Sadie standing with her hands on her hips. "What?" I said stupidly.

"That's not how the rhyme goes," Sadie repeated. "You're doing it wrong."

The happiness whooshed out of me like air from a popped balloon.

"We're making up our own words," Isabel explained. "It's fun."

I straightened my spine to remind myself I had one. "What are you now, the playground police?" I said.

Sadie huffed. "No. I just thought you'd want to know you got the words wrong. Everyone can hear you and you're saying it wrong and it sounds dumb. I'm trying to do you a favor."

Some favor. I ignored her and turned to Isabel. I could be just as mean as Sadie was. I'd give her a taste of her own medicine. "Did you hear something?" I said.

Isabel looked at Sadie then at me. She blinked. "Um, yes?"

"Well, I didn't," I said. "I didn't hear anything that matters. Just the wind whistling across the playground."

Sadie opened her mouth to snap at me, but I

cut her off. "Hey, Sadie, do you know this one?" I swung my jump rope and jumped hard. "One, two, no one likes you. Three, four, not anymore."

Sadie's eyes popped. She looked as shocked as if I'd spit in her face. I kept going. "Five, six, this you can't fix. Seven, eight, you're full of hate."

Two fat tears rolled down Sadie's cheeks. I couldn't believe it. I was making her cry.

I stopped jumping.

This felt terrible. I wanted to throw up, or to hug Sadie and apologize, to say I didn't mean it, but I forced my face into a smile instead and tried to remind myself that Sadie deserved it. She'd stolen my necklace and stopped being my friend. She'd acted super mean and even threatened to take Banana. I was only fighting back, like Chuck said I should.

"Anna," Isabel said softly. "What's going on?"

I crossed my arms over the hurt in my chest. "Ask the necklace thief," I said.

Sadie didn't look sad any longer. Now she looked furious. She looked so mad, I thought fire might come out her nostrils. "Whatever," she said. "It's a stupid baby necklace anyway. I don't even want it." Sadie grabbed my necklace, ripped it off her neck with one sharp yank, and threw it on the ground.

I gasped and reached for it, but before I could rescue it, Sadie stomped it into the dirt. She turned and marched off, curls bouncing.

I was too stunned to breathe.

Isabel picked up my necklace and rubbed off the dirt until the pendant was shining again.

"Pretty," she said. She dropped it into my hand. I couldn't even look at the ruined chain. I couldn't believe Sadie had done that. And I couldn't believe what I'd done to Sadie. The things I'd said had been awful. "Maybe it can be fixed," Isabel said.

I shoved the necklace into the pocket of my skirt. I didn't want to think about everything that was broken. "Who cares," I said. "C'mon, let's do one about places." I skipped over my rope. "One, two, Kalamazoo!"

I kept jumping and jumping and jumping and didn't once look behind me for Sadie or wish she'd come back.

Chapter Fifteen

Lots to Chew On

"How was school?" my dad asked that night as he heaped spaghetti onto everyone's dinner plates. It smelled delicious.

"Fine," Chuck mumbled around a hunk of garlic bread.

"Charles, no talking with your mouth full, please," Mom said. "And would you care to share a few more details?"

Chuck swallowed. "Nope," he said, and stuffed in another bite.

"I'll share," I said. "This morning in art I drew a really pretty unicorn. Even Isabel said it was good,

and she's the best artist in our whole class. We played jump rope at recess and made up our own rhymes, and at lunch she taught me how to say 'My name is Anna' in Spanish. *Me llamo Anna.*"

Dad looked impressed. "Cool," he said.

"Yeah," I agreed. "Isabel is great. She let me use her sparkly pen all through social studies, and she has a cat that's as big as Banana, and her sister plays cello in the middle-school orchestra."

My mom reached for the salad dressing. "Wow," she said. "And do Isabel and Sadie get along well too?"

I shrugged and twirled a few strands of spaghetti around my fork. Suddenly it didn't look so tasty. "Who cares? Sadie's not my friend."

"She isn't?" Dad said. "Since when?"

Uh-oh. I shouldn't have said that. I did *not* want to talk about it. I shoved the pasta into my mouth and pointed to show I couldn't answer while chewing.

"Since she stole Anna's birthday necklace," Chuck answered for me.

"Chuck!" I shouted, spraying little bits of tomato sauce onto my lap. Banana looked up at them hopefully. She always spends dinnertime under the table, waiting for food to drop.

Dad put down his utensils. His face looked serious. "What's that? Sadie took something from you?"

I stared at my plate. "No. Sort of. Maybe. It doesn't matter. Anyway, I got it back." *Please don't ask to see it, please don't ask to see it,* I begged silently. I didn't want my parents to know the necklace was broken. Then I'd be in even bigger trouble than I was in now.

Mom put a hand on my shoulder. "Anna, what's this about? Do we need to call Sadie's mom or Ms. Burland to help you two work it out?"

"No!" I said, horrified. "Then she'll think I'm a tattletale!"

"It's not tattling to talk to your parents about something that's upsetting you," my dad said, as if he had never been a kid himself.

I hunched over my dinner and wished I could disappear, or at least slide off my chair to hide under the table with Banana. Even being down near Chuck's stinky feet and eating crumbs off the floor would be better than this. "Nothing's upsetting me," I said. "I already told you, my day was great. I don't need Sadie and I don't even miss her and everything is totally fine."

I didn't look at my parents or Chuck or even Banana, because I didn't want to know if they could tell I was lying.

I did miss Sadie. I missed her a lot.

Chapter Sixteen
Tucking in, Tuckered Out

I tucked myself into bed early and stared up at the ceiling, listening to Banana's piglet-like snores and thinking about my ex–best friend. I couldn't believe she was really ditching me. I couldn't believe we would never spend another Saturday spying on her neighbor Mrs. Greene through the fence between their backyards, making up the other sides of the phone calls Mrs. Greene had while she sunbathed. Sadie was really good at that. And she was great at inventing funny rules we had to follow, like the day when we were only allowed to walk on our tiptoes, or the time we spoke in rhymes for an entire sleepover. I didn't mind that Sadie could be bossy sometimes. Usually the things she said we had to do turned out to be really fun.

But now Sadie didn't want to be my friend anymore. It made me sad and it made me angry, but also, it made me confused. I knew Sadie wasn't really a meanie inside, so I didn't understand why she'd acted like one.

Even becoming friends with Isabel couldn't fix this. I still had a Sadie-size hole in my heart.

Banana woke up and thumped her tail against her basket as Mom pushed open my bedroom door and light from the hallway flooded in. Mom sat on the edge of my bed and the mattress sank a little under her weight. I let it roll me toward her so we could cuddle.

Mom patted my back. Her silver bracelets clinked together. I felt myself melt a little under her touch. "Do you want to talk about what happened with Sadie?" she asked.

I shut my eyes and realized the answer was yes. "I was just trying to stand up for myself," I said. "She's been hating me all week and I don't even know why. But now she has a good reason, because today I was mean and horrible right back."

I waited for a lecture about being nice, and

how you don't have to bully back to defend yourself. Mom stayed quiet and her hand kept moving in slow circles on my back. Maybe she didn't understand how bad things were.

"I made Sadie cry," I confessed. "It felt terrible."

"Hmm," Mom said.

I sniffed. "Everything's ruined."

"Maybe. Maybe not," she said. "I think Sadie loves you a lot, but I'd guess that sometimes she also feels a little jealous of you."

I opened my eyes fast. "Jealous of me? No way. Sadie has everything. Her parents both buy her whatever she wants, and she's allowed to drink soda and watch TV all the time. She doesn't even have a bedtime. She definitely doesn't have a chore wheel."

"True," Mom said. "But just as you sometimes wish your life could be more like Sadie's, maybe sometimes Sadie wishes she had some of the things you have, like a big brother and parents who are still together."

"Well, she can have Chuck," I mumbled.

Mom ignored that. "Anyway, it's great that you made a new friend," she said. "Isabel sounds terrific and your dad and I can't wait to meet her. And maybe what you and Sadie need is a little break from each other right now. But it's possible to have more than one friend, you know."

"But not more than one *best* friend," I said.

"Sure it is," Mom said. "Like how I have two favorite children. You're both the best, but in different ways."

"Really?" I asked.

"Really," she said.

I sat up. "But what if you *had* to choose between us? Like, if Chuck and I fell off a dock, who would you jump in and save from drowning?"

"I'd save you both, silly," Mom said.

I rolled my eyes. "But if you could only grab one of us."

Mom squeezed my hand. "Then I'd rescue Banana, because Banana hates the water and I know I raised both of my children to swim."

"Hmph." I flopped back against my pillow and pretended to pout, but I was secretly glad that Mom thinks I'm strong enough to rescue myself. It's true, I am a really good swimmer.

Mom pulled the blankets up tight under my chin how I like them. "I wish I could save you from feeling sad about Sadie," she said. "But I bet you'll figure out how to swim through this, too." She kissed my forehead. "Good night, Annabear."

"Good night, Mamabear," I said back.

I was asleep before she even shut the door.

Chapter Seventeen
Giddyup

Sunlight streamed through the kitchen window the next morning as I gave Banana her breakfast and poured myself a big bowl of Gorilla Grams with milk.

Chuck leaned over. "Hey, Anna," he said. "What's brown and smells like bananas?"

"What?" I asked.

"Gorilla poop!" Chuck said. He laughed at his own joke.

I nodded. That was funny, but I could do better. "Hey, Chuck," I said. "What's invisible and smells like Banana?"

Chuck looked at me sideways. "What?" he said.

"Doggy farts," I answered.

Chuck snorted. "Nice one." We smirked at each other.

Dad was whistling as he walked into the kitchen. He picked up his TOP DOG coffee mug. "Good morning, kiddos," he said. "Ready to face the day?"

"I'm ready to *butt* the day," Chuck said.

I groaned. That didn't even make sense.

"Hey, Dad?" I said, feeling brave. "Do you think maybe you could help me with something?"

"I could certainly try," Dad said. "What is it?"

Banana's ears perked up in surprise as I pulled the broken birthday necklace out of my pocket. "This," I said.

Dad took the necklace from my hand and examined it. He held it so close to his eye that if the pony had come alive in that moment, it could have swished at his cheek with its tail.

I held my breath.

"Hmm," Dad said. "Looks like some of the little links in the chain snapped apart somehow, and this other one is twisted. But I bet if we just . . ." He was already taking his pliers out of a drawer. Hope raced up my spine.

A few minutes later, Dad fastened the necklace around my neck. "There," he said. "See what you think."

I jumped off the breakfast stool and ran to a mirror. The pony pendant shimmered and pranced in the reflection, beneath my huge grin.

It looked brand-new again—just like magic.

I hugged Dad and hugged Banana. Problem fixed.

"I wish I could use Dad's pliers to fix things with Sadie," I whispered into Banana's fur. Banana gave me sad a look and I knew she was right: It wouldn't work for Sadie and me to be squeezed back together. Sadie would have to want to fix us too.

Chapter Eighteen
Wishful Thinking

I got to school a little bit early, and Isabel was waiting for me on the playground. Sadie was nowhere in sight.

Isabel grabbed my hand. "C'mon!" she said. "I want to teach you a new game."

The game was like hopscotch mixed with freeze tag—"stop-hop," Isabel called it—and we played it until the first bell rang. We even let Justin and Timothy play too, though they weren't as good at it as we were. Timothy kept jumping when he was supposed to freeze and freezing when he was supposed to jump. Justin kept falling over on purpose to make us all laugh.

When we got to class, Sadie was already in her seat with her nose in a book. She didn't look up until Ms. Burland clapped twice to start the day. But even then, Sadie didn't look over at me. She just stared straight ahead at the whiteboard, where Ms. Burland had already written the word of the day: *far-fetched*. That sounded like a word Banana would like. I pictured her scampering after a far-flung ball and fetching it to bring proudly back to me. I read the definition: *unlikely or seemingly impossible*.

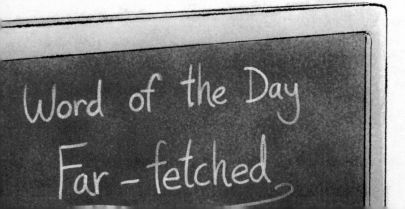

Far-fetched. I touched the necklace at my throat and remembered how impossible it had seemed that I would ever get to wear it again.

While Ms. Burland explained how we were going to build models of the solar system out of Styrofoam balls and wire and paint, I snuck another glance at Sadie. This time, her eyes met mine. She turned away quickly, before I could even react. When I looked again, her face was hard to read, but I let myself pretend that she secretly missed me too.

Maybe if Isabel and I played stop-hop again at recess, Sadie would walk by and we could invite her to play with us. She would probably really like Isabel's games. She'd probably also like Isabel. We wouldn't have to make a big deal over apologizing and making up and stuff. We could just start playing together and soon everything would go back to normal. Except it would be better than normal, because we would have Isabel to hang out with too.

I got so excited thinking about how well that plan would work, that by the time recess started, it already felt like a sure thing. Isabel and I raced out to the playground and claimed the perfect patch of pavement for our game. We played the whole recess and I kept watching for Sadie to come near, but I didn't see her. Not even once.

Maybe my mom was right. Maybe Sadie wanted a break from being friends with me. Maybe I needed to give her some time. But it already felt like we'd been un-friends forever.

Chapter Nineteen
The Sparkle Surprise

The bell rang for the end of recess and kids ran toward the building, wanting to be first in line for hot lunch. Isabel and I walked, since we'd both brought our lunches from home. We stopped in the classroom to get them.

Ms. Burland sat at the front of the room, with her sandwich in one hand and a book in the other. I smiled at her and headed toward my desk, then froze. I couldn't believe what I saw.

Sitting on my desktop, lined up where I'd left them, were my regular yellow pencil and my lucky blue one. But beneath the blue one was something unexpected. Something impossible. It was a sparkly rainbow pencil, just like the one I'd stepped on three days ago, after eating Sadie's note. But my favorite special pencil had been broken in two that awful day. This pencil was brand-new and perfect, and definitely hadn't been on my desk when I'd left for recess. I stared, almost expecting it to vanish before my eyes.

"What's wrong?" Isabel asked, noticing I wasn't moving.

I shook off my surprise. "That pencil," I said. "With the rainbows. Did you put it there?"

"Nope," Isabel said. "Wasn't me."

I looked over at Ms. Burland. She shook her head and shrugged. "Must have been the pencil fairy," she said. "Go on, grab your lunch."

A hurricane of feelings stormed through my chest as I picked up my lunch bag and followed Isabel out of the classroom, leaving the new pencil behind. I was almost afraid to let myself think it, but I knew the pencil was from Sadie. It *had* to be.

Even though she still wasn't speaking to me, maybe she didn't want our friendship to be broken either. Maybe, just maybe, Sadie was sorry too.

Chapter Twenty
As You Wish

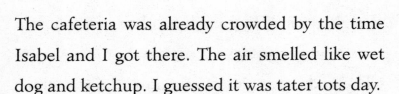

The cafeteria was already crowded by the time Isabel and I got there. The air smelled like wet dog and ketchup. I guessed it was tater tots day.

Isabel swung her lunchbox while we looked around for a good place to sit. I was eyeing two seats near some kids I sort of knew from Mr. Garrison's class when I spotted Sadie across the room. She was sitting alone at a table by the windows, taking everything out of her lunchbox and arranging it all neatly in front of her. Sadie likes things organized, even her lunch. Once, we made a game of organizing all of Banana's toys by size and shape and squeakiness, while Banana made a game of un-organizing them back into a mess. Remembering how much fun Sadie, Banana, and I always had, I knew I had to try talking to her one last time. She looked like she was still ignoring me, but the pencil had given me hope.

"C'mon," I said to Isabel, and before I could lose my nerve, I led the way to Sadie's table.

My heart thudded like a kick drum as we walked over, but I reminded myself I had nothing left to lose. "Can we sit here?" I asked.

Sadie looked surprised. She didn't smile, but she didn't make a mean face, either. "I guess so," she said.

Isabel had already slid onto the bench across from her. "Is that peanut butter and banana?" she asked, looking at Sadie's sandwich, which was the same kind her mom's housekeeper always packed. "Lucky," Isabel added. "I think I got turkey again."

Sadie lit up. "Turkey! Let's trade halves."

I sat down next to Isabel while she and Sadie made the switch. I opened up my lunch and saw that Dad had packed two treats: a granola bar and a box of raisins. Sadie and I love raisins.

I pushed the box toward Sadie. "You want some?" I asked.

For a second, Sadie looked at the raisins like she thought they might be booby-trapped. Then she popped a few into her mouth. "Thanks," she said. "You can have my applesauce if you want." Her voice was all mischief.

I made a face. "Ew. No thanks." I love apples, but I hate applesauce. Once, Sadie and I wrote a funny poem about the way it squishes and oozes like a slug in your mouth.

I bit into my cheese sandwich and almost choked when Sadie shouted, "Hey!" She was so loud, a few kids at other tables turned to gawk at us. Sadie was staring at my neck. "You fixed our necklace!" she said.

I took a deep breath. "*My* necklace," I said.

I looked straight at Sadie and didn't blink. I wanted us to be friends, but she had to know I wasn't going to let her push me around.

Sadie blushed. "Right," she said.

A wave of gladness washed over me. "I might let you borrow it again sometime," I offered, then added, "if you're nice."

She nodded. "Thanks," she said.

And just like that, I knew we'd be okay. I couldn't wait to tell Banana.

I turned to Isabel. "It's my birthday necklace," I explained. "It's kinda magic. I got it after I blew out my candles and wished for a pony."

"Which was my idea," Sadie added.

"It was a good idea," I said. Sadie beamed.

"That's so cool," Isabel said. "I never know

what to wish for. But I've already decided what I want for my party."

"What?" Sadie asked.

"Well, my sisters and I all love waterslides, so usually we take a family trip to Water World," Isabel said.

"Wow." I couldn't help feeling a little jealous. I tried not to show it.

Isabel looked shyly at Sadie and me. "But I'm thinking maybe this year I'll ask to invite friends. I mean, if you'd want to—"

"YES!" I shouted, before Isabel could even finish the sentence. She and Sadie laughed, and I realized I'd jumped right out of my seat. I sat back down. "I mean," I said, "that sounds amazing."

I pictured the three of us zooming down a

giant waterslide, splashing and shrieking and grinning our heads off. It would be twice as fun going there with two best friends. *Everything* would be twice as fun, and probably three times more interesting. I couldn't have wished for a happier ending.

Acknowledgments

Heaps of thanks to editor Kristin Ostby, designer Laurent Linn, illustrator Meg Park, and the whole fantastic team at S&S.

Bouquets of gratitude to Robin Wasserman, Terra Elan McVoy, Andrew Garrison, Lauren Strasnick, and Lucy Simonoff.

Appreciation and adoration galore for my agent, Meredith Kaffel.

Hugs to Grammy Mrose, Auntie Sue, NiNo, the original Chuck, and my wonderful parents.

And a heart drawn with glitter glue for you, reader.

And now, a sneak peek at the next book
in the series, *ANNA, BANANA, AND
THE MONKEY IN THE MIDDLE!*

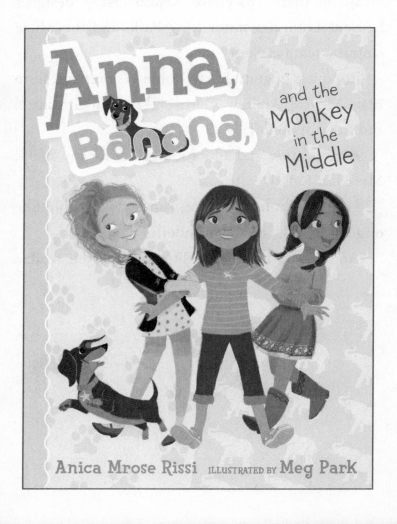

I popped up like a jackrabbit-in-the-box, feeling wide-awake and eager as a beaver. I had animals on the brain.

"Banana!" I said, leaning over the side of my bed. "We're going to the zoo!"

Banana looked up at me with her big doggy eyes and thumped her tail against the pillow in her basket where she sleeps. I reached down to tug her soft ears. She understood, of course, that by "we" I didn't mean her and me—dogs aren't allowed on school field trips. I meant me and my best friends, Sadie and Isabel, plus the rest of our class and the other two third-grade classes. It was going to be a super fun day.

"I wish I could sneak you there in my backpack," I said. "Then you could meet the prairie dogs!"

My teacher, Ms. Burland, had shown us pictures of prairie dogs and some of the other animals we'd be seeing at the zoo. We'd learned what the animals eat and how they play and other cool things about them. I liked hearing about the animals' habitats, like where they sleep and what parts of the world they're from. Ms. Burland says the animals that live in a place are part of what makes that region unique. ("Unique" had been our word of the day. It means special and different and one of a kind.) That made a lot of sense to me. Banana definitely makes my house unique, and my room is extra special because she sleeps there.

"But actually," I told her as I slid out of bed, "prairie dogs are in the squirrel family, not the dog family. So if I took you to the zoo, you'd probably want to chase them."

Banana wiggled in agreement. She loves chasing squirrels.

"They're called prairie dogs because they bark like dogs," I said. "And because they live in the prairie. Except for the ones that live at the zoo."

Banana yawned and stretched her front legs. I guess she'd heard enough facts about prairie dogs.

I made my bed and pulled on my outfit of black leggings, a pink-and-white striped shirt, pink sneakers, and black-and-white polka-dot socks. While I got dressed, I sang a silly song that Isabel had made up. "We're going to the zoo! A-doob-a-doob-a-doo! We're going to the zoo! You and me and you!" Yesterday at recess, Isabel and I had linked arms and skipped around the playground, belting out the song at the top of our lungs. We'd stopped short when I'd noticed Sadie watching us with her arms crossed and her eyebrows worried. We hadn't meant to leave Sadie out. It had just happened. Luckily, Isabel had grabbed on to Sadie and soon we were all three skipping and singing, and Sadie looked happy again. But it had been a close call.

Sadie and I have been friends forever, but we only just met Isabel this year. It's twice as much fun having two best friends, and mostly, we all get along great. But in some ways Sadie and Isabel are still getting used to each other, I think. I was glad we would have the whole day at the zoo to have fun as a threesome. Banana and I were certain that by the end of the field trip, Sadie and Isabel would be calling each other "best friend" too.